Ready, Set, Go!

by Suzanne Hardin
illustrated by Marjorie Scott

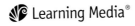
Learning Media®

Contents

1. House for Sale

"How's it going in there?" Bailey's mom called from the hallway.

"Not so good," answered Bailey.

"Would you like some help?" Mom asked. "The sooner your room is clean, the sooner you can go and play."

"No, it's OK, Mom," said Bailey. "There's no one to play with anyway."

"All right, then. I'll be downstairs doing the laundry if you need me," said Mom.

Bailey finished cleaning her room. She put some things in her craft bin, then she went outside to empty her wastebasket.

As she put the lid back on the trash can, a car pulled up in front of the house next door. The house had been for sale for a long time.

Bailey hoped that a family with children had come to look at the house. But an older man got out of the car. He shook hands with the real estate agent, and they went inside the house.

A few days later, Bailey noticed a SOLD sign in the front yard.

"*Another* neighbor without any kids," she thought.

2. A New Project

On Saturday morning, Bailey woke up to the sound of a pounding hammer. "What's making all that noise?" she grumbled. She sat up in bed and looked out the window.

A carpenter was building a ramp up to the porch of the house next door. Bailey watched him for a while. Then she got up and went downstairs for breakfast.

At breakfast, Mom emptied the last of the juice into Bailey's glass. Then she threw the juice box into the trash.

"Hey! I can use that!" Bailey jumped up and grabbed the juice box. Bailey liked to make things, and the juice box had given her an idea.

"Wait a minute," said Mom. "You haven't finished your pancakes yet."

Bailey finished her breakfast as quickly as she could.

She washed the juice box, then went to her craft bin. She rooted around until she found what she was looking for.

Bailey began to work on her new project. She made four slots in the corners of the box. Then she pushed pencils through the slots, and she pushed paper cup lids onto the ends of the pencils.

Bailey sat back and looked at what she had made.

3. The Boy

Later in the week, Bailey saw the older man talking to some men in a moving van. He smiled and waved at her. Bailey waved back. She thought he looked nice enough, but she still wished that a family with kids had moved in.

On Saturday morning, Bailey saw a boy sitting on the front porch of the house next door.

"He must be visiting his grandfather," Bailey thought. She wanted to talk to him, but she felt a bit shy.

Later that day, Bailey saw the boy's grandfather on the porch. He helped the boy into a car, and they drove away.

Bailey wondered where they were going. Perhaps he was taking the boy home.

4. An Idea

On Sunday afternoon, Bailey decided to make some changes to her juice-box racer. First she removed the wheels and colored them blue. Then she traced around the sides of the box onto bright paper. She cut this out and glued the colorful paper onto the juice box. Then she put the wheels back on.

Bailey took the racer downstairs to try it out on the kitchen floor.

When she gave the car a little shove, it moved but not very far. "What's *wrong* with you?" Bailey said crossly.

Mom looked up from her book. "What's wrong with *you*, Bailey? Why are you so cranky?"

Bailey didn't answer. She just sighed.
She was tired of playing by herself, but
she thought Mom wouldn't understand.

Bailey sat the juice-box racer on the
counter. She got a drink of water.
Looking out the window, she could see
the boy. He was sitting all by himself.
He didn't seem to have anything to do.

Bailey had an idea.

5. Making Friends

Bailey grabbed a few things from her craft bin. She stuffed them into a paper sack along with her juice-box racer.

"I'm going to see the boy next door, Mom," she called.

"OK, honey. The fresh air will do you good," replied Mom.

Bailey walked across the yard to the house next door. "Hi," she said shyly. "I'm Bailey."

"Hi, I'm Nate," the boy said. He looked at Bailey's puffy paper sack. "What's in your bag?"

Bailey pulled out her juice-box racer.
Nate looked at it carefully. "Does it
really go?" he asked.

"Yes, but it still needs some work,"
Bailey replied.

Bailey gave the car a push. It wobbled across the porch. "See what I mean," she said.

"Let me take a look. I think I know what the problem is," said Nate. "These back wheels are rubbing against the sides. Try moving them out a little."

Bailey moved the wheels out. Her racer moved a lot faster.

"Thanks for the tip," she said. "Do you want to make your own juice-box racer?"

"Sure," Nate answered, "but where would I get all the stuff to make one?"

"Don't worry about that," Bailey replied.
"I brought everything you need, just in
case you were interested."

6. Ready to Race

Bailey showed Nate how to make a juice-box racer like hers. He colored the wheels and covered his box with foil. They added decorations to both their cars.

Bailey made a rainbow shape. Then she colored it and glued it onto the top of her racer.

Nate folded thin strips of paper back and forth and taped them onto his car. Then he made two signs that said THUNDERBOLT and put them on the sides.

When the racers were ready, Nate said, "Let's use the ramp to try them out."

Nate sat near the top of the ramp and let the cars go while Bailey stayed at the bottom to pick the cars up.

"Why don't we time our racers," said
Nate. "I've got a stopwatch."

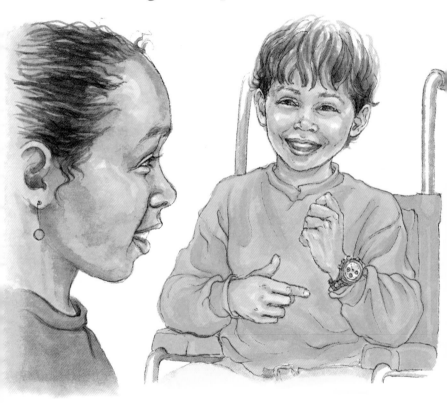

"Sure," Bailey said. So they timed their
racers and spent the rest of the afternoon
trying to go faster in each race.

7. A Nice Surprise

"Bailey, where are you?" called Bailey's mom.

"Over here," Bailey waved.

"I need you to come home to set the table for supper," said Mom.

"Do I have to?" Bailey replied.

Mom was pleased to see Bailey having fun. "OK," she said. "Five more minutes."

Nate looked at Bailey. "Do you want to have one final race to see whose car is the fastest?" he asked.

"Great!" Bailey answered.

Bailey wished she had someone like Nate to play with all the time.

"So, how long are you visiting your grandpa for?" she asked.

"Visiting?" Nate said in surprise. "Didn't you know? I live with my grandpa."

"Really?" A big smile spread across Bailey's face.

"I guess that makes us neighbors," said Nate. He grinned back at her. "Now, let's race!"

"Ready, set, go!" yelled Nate. As the
juice-box racers zoomed down the ramp,
Bailey didn't really care whose car came
first. She was just glad to have a friend
next door.

How to Make a Juice-box Racer

You need:

1 juice box   scissors
2 pencils   decorations
4 paper cup lids   glue

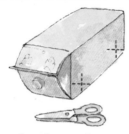

1. Make four slots in the corners of the box.

2. Push the pencils through the slots.

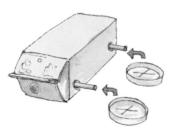

3. Push the lids onto the ends of the pencils, leaving gaps between the sides of the box and the lids.

4. Decorate your juice-box racer.